To Marc, Yuna, Adriel
and their incredible ideas.

Susanna Isern

To my Dad, who was full of enthusiasm and
fantastic ideas, and who will always be in my heart.

Sonja Wimmer

Bogo, The Fox Who Wanted Everything
Somos8 Series

© Text: Susanna Isern, 2015
© Illustration: Sonja Wimmer, 2015
© Edition: NubeOcho, 2015
www.nubeocho.com – info@nubeocho.com

Original title: *Bogo Quierelotodo*
English translation: Martin Hyams
Text editing: Caroline Dookie

Distributed in the United States by
Consortium Book Sales & Distribution

First edition: 2016
ISBN: 978-84-944446-6-1
Printed in China

Bogo
The Fox
Who Wanted
Everything

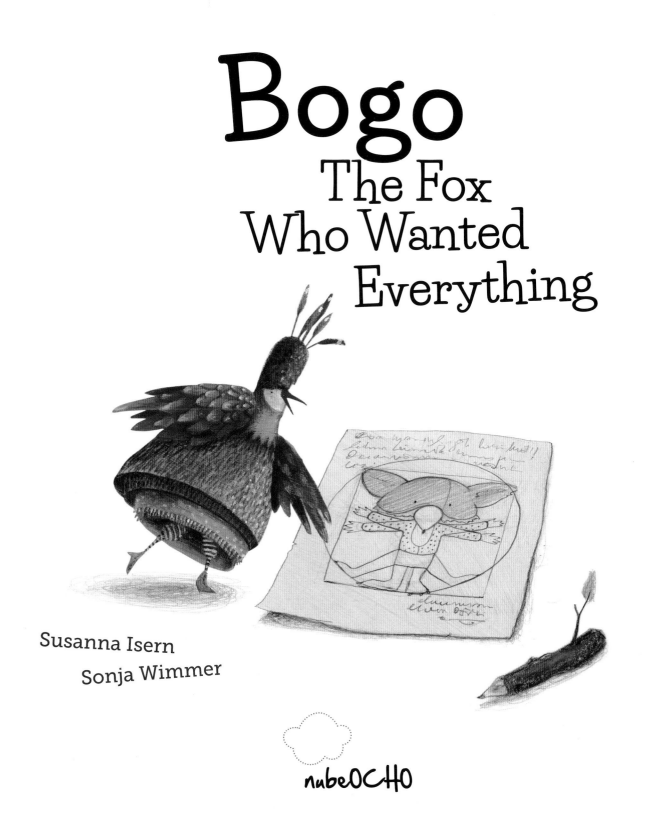

Susanna Isern

Sonja Wimmer

nubeOCHO

Bogo the fox lived in the branches of a great big tree.

This is quite unusual for a fox, but he was a **very curious** fox and from up there he could see everything much better.

Bogo watched everything around him.
Many animals lived in the forest, and some of them were so **incredible** that they made Bogo feel less special.

One day he decided to invent amazing things so that he could have everything he wanted.

Bogo's **first invention** was a pair of **wings** to fly like a **bird**.

He used a variety of twigs and feathers, including feathers from an eagle, or so he was assured by **Patty, the swooping swallow.**

But with or without eagle feathers, that invention was a disaster.

As soon as Bogo started to flap his wings, he **crashed** with such a **bump** that he lost three **teeth** and twisted his **tail**.

Oh Bogo!
You can't have everything!

Who ever heard of
a fox that can fly!

Bogo's **second invention** was
a pair of **night glasses** to see
like an **owl** on a moonless night.

He used glass made of **bat tears,**
or so he was assured by **Lolo,
the bear** that hibernated in the
darkest caves.

But with or without **bat tears,** the invention was a flop.

With his first step in the **dark,** Bogo ran into a pot, fell into the river and caught a bad cold.

Oh Bogo!
You can't have everything!

Who ever heard of **a fox with glasses!**

His **third invention** was a pair of jumping **stilts** to leap as high as a **frog.** But despite using **fantastic springs,** this invention didn't work out either.

The first time Bogo jumped, he **crashed** into a tree and knocked himself out.

Oh Bogo!
You can't have everything!

Who ever heard of a fox
who could jump as high as a frog!

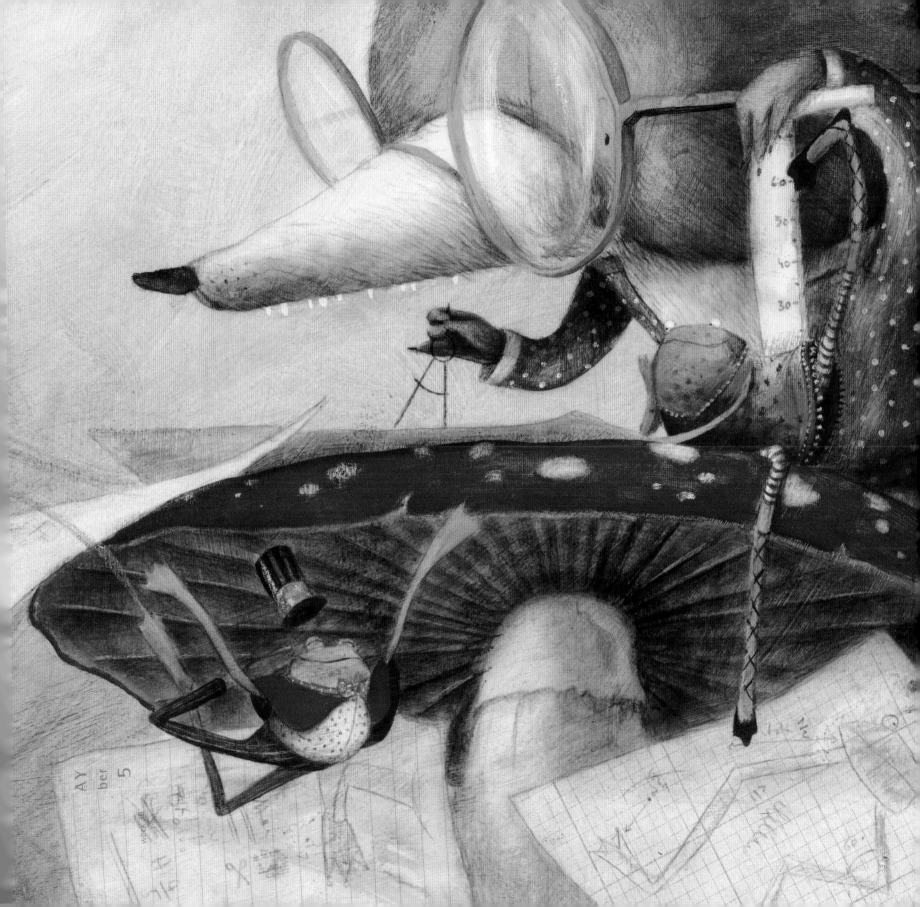

The fourth invention was a **shell** for protection, just like a **turtle's shell**. But despite using rock powder, that invention went wrong too.

With the first gust of wind, the shell **collapsed** and Bogo got so much sand up his nose that made him sneeze all night long.

Oh Bogo!
You can't have everything!

Who ever heard of a fox
with a shell!

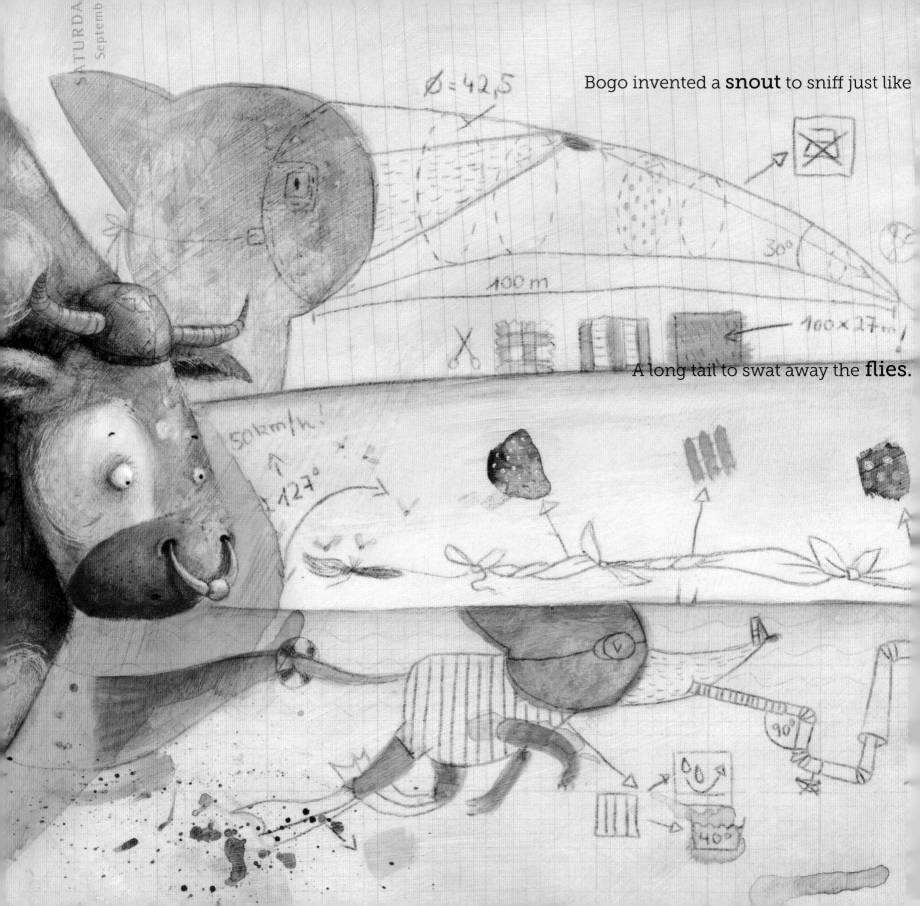

an **anteater.** It never worked.

He **tried** it out and it fell off.

← 30m

And even a tube for breathing under water like a **fish.** He swallowed half the river trying that out.

Oh Bogo!
You can't have everything!

Who ever heard of a fox
that could do all those things!

There were so many **failed inventions** that Bogo decided to stop trying. He felt that he was not special and would never be. And he was **so sad** that he spent his days at home, not even looking out the window.

The forest animals were worried about him and they missed his **weird ideas**.

One night, a pack of wolves arrived **silently** in the forest. Bogo, who was sleeping with the window open, smelled them immediately:

"Wolf pack, if I'm not mistaken, I smell a mouse, a turtle, a big bear and many other delicacies" whispered the leader of the pack, **licking his lips**.

Quickly and quietly, Bogo warned the animals to hide in a **safe place**.

The wolves looked up in the most unlikely **corners** of the forest, but all the animals were all so well **hidden** that they found nothing. When the day dawned, the wolves left with **empty bellies**.

The next morning everyone was talking about what had happened last night:

"How did you know the wolves were here?"

"I smelled them." **Oh Bogo!**

Your fox's **nose** is such

an amazing invention!

"How did you know they wanted to eat us?"
"I heard them **whispering.**"

Oh Bogo!
Your fox's **ears** are such
an **amazing invention!**

"How come you came to tell us?"
"I had to!"
Oh Bogo!
Your fox's **cunning** is such
an **amazing invention!**

"And how did you manage to tell us without being discovered?"
"I ran as **fast** as I could, trying not to make a noise!"

Oh Bogo!

Your fox's **legs** are such

an **amazing invention!**

That's when Bogo **realized** that he
also had a lot of special qualities.

Ever since then, even though his
crazy inventions never worked,
Bogo carried on **inventing** because
it was something he loved doing.

Oh Bogo!
Never change!

we love your **crazy ideas**!